First Animals Book

Turn to page 39 to discover how sandgrouse collect water in the desert.
Turn to page 25 to find out how to spot moths at night.
What colour do I turn in winter? Find out on page 36.
Find out why many ocean fish swim in schools on page 42.
Learn some strange names for animal groups on page 29.

First Animals Book

Barbara Taylor

Consultant: Anne Rooney

Illustrated by Diane Ewen and Nila Aye

SCHOLASTIC

Contents

I'm built to survive the freezing Antarctic.

I get my colour from my food!

I'm using this shell to protect my soft body.

All kinds of animals

Animals come in all shapes and sizes, from tiny ants to enormous whales. People are animals too! Scientists think there are nearly 8 million different kinds of animal on Earth. Each kind is called a species.

Looking inside

Scientists divide animals into two huge groups. Animals with a backbone are called **vertebrates**. Animals with no backbone are called **invertebrates**.

Invertebrates

Most animals (97 percent) are invertebrates. Some have a hard shell or outer skeleton.

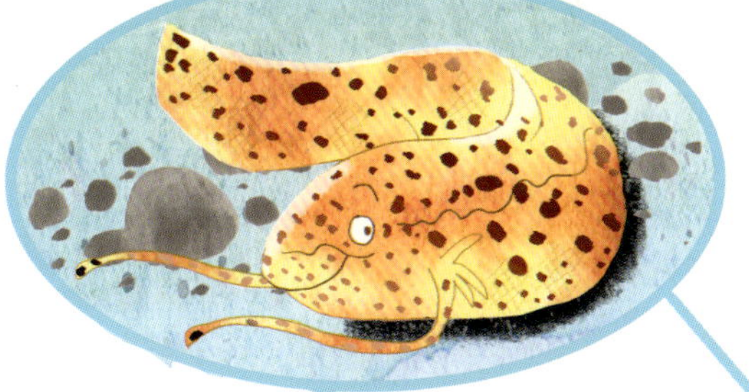

Vertebrates

Vertebrates are split into five smaller groups: mammals, birds, reptiles, amphibians and fishes.

Sponges are animals too!

An ostrich's eye is bigger than its brain!

Animals have certain things in common. They eat other living things. They use their senses to find food and move around to get it.

I CAN... CHOOSE MY FAVOURITE ANIMAL

Think about your favourite animal. Look through this book to help you decide which to choose. Why do you like this animal? What does it eat? How fast does it move? Which senses help it to survive?

Big and small

The biggest animals in the world are huge whales in the oceans. The blue whale is the biggest animal ever! Yet it feeds on tiny, shrimp-like creatures called krill. There is enough space and food on Earth for small animals to thrive in vast numbers.

A blue whale can be up to 30 metres long. Its heart is the size of a small car!

I CAN... PAINT AN ATLAS MOTH

Take a piece of paper, fold it in half and then open it out flat. Paint one of the moth's wings and half its body to the left of the fold line. Then fold the paper again and press down to make the other half. Open it up to see your moth.

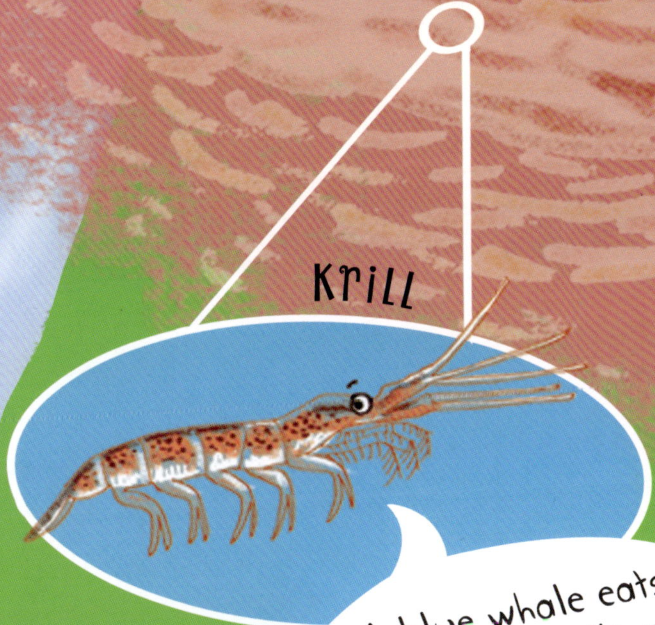

Huge appetite

The African elephant is the largest animal on land. It's up to 7 metres long and weighs up to 7 tonnes. An elephant spends about 16 hours a day eating!

Coats and armour

You are a hairy animal, just like other mammals. Other animal groups have different body coverings. Birds have feathers, amphibians have smooth skin, and reptiles and most fish have scales.

Skin suit

An animal's skin is like a waterproof suit, which protects its body from damage and disease.

Always in armour

Scales made from hard skin, or horn, protect the bodies of some animals like suits of armour.

I CAN... MAKE A SCALY SCENE

Create an underwater scene. Draw some fish onto card and cut them out. Glue small pieces of coloured paper and kitchen foil onto each fish to create spectacular scaly skin. Stick your fish onto a shiny blue piece of paper and decorate the background.

Hide and seek

Colours and patterns help some animals to play hide and seek! Others use them to stand out from the crowd.

In plain sight

Many animals that are good at hiding from predators have colours or patterns that match their background. This is called camouflage.

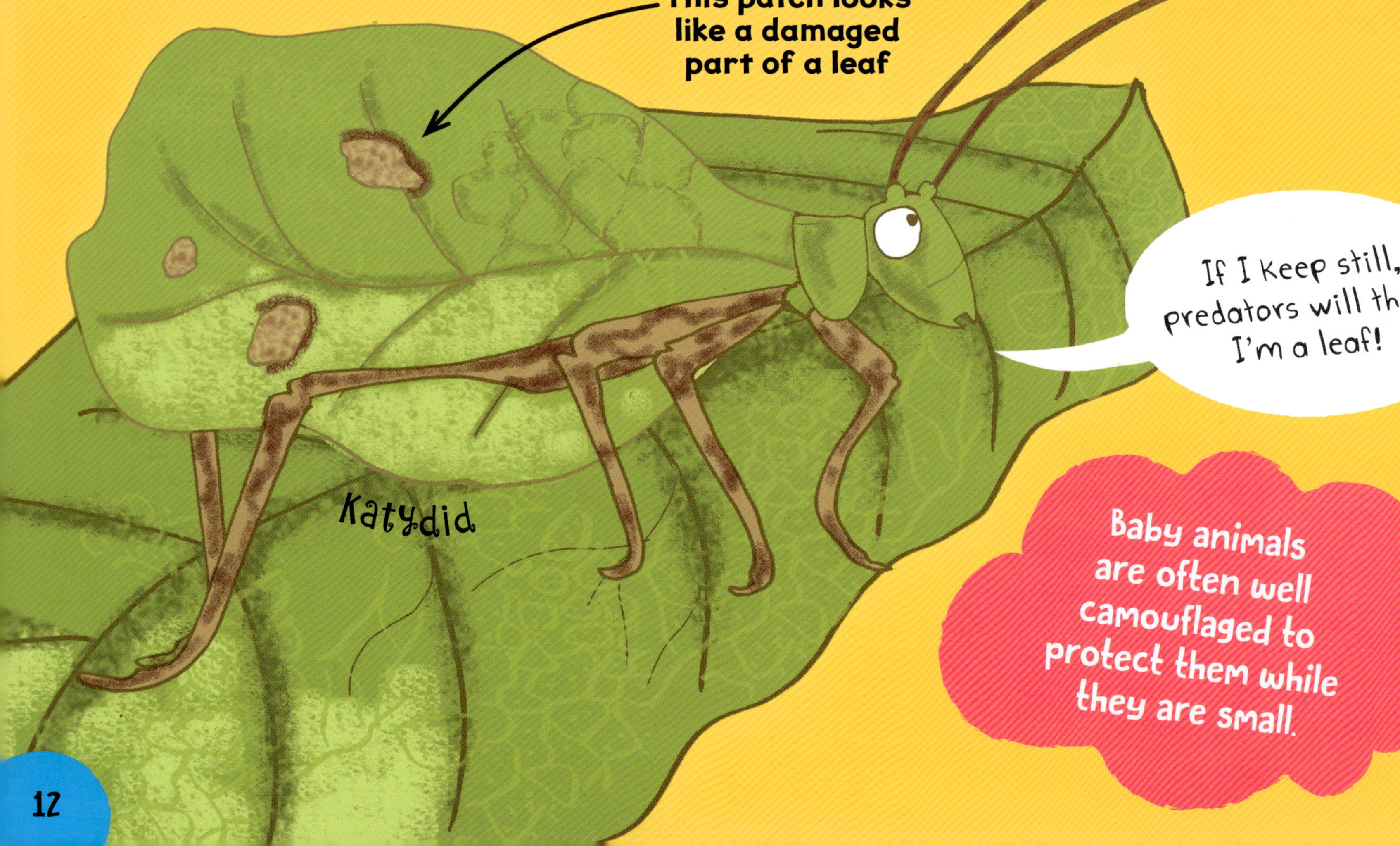

Baby animals are often well camouflaged to protect them while they are small.

Don't eat me!

Animals that are poisonous or taste nasty often have bright colours to warn predators not to eat them.

I CAN... USE CAMOUFLAGE

Make a camouflage headband to hide against a leafy background. Cut a strip of card and paint it green, brown or black. Glue leaves and grass on top and fix the ends around your head with sticky tape.

Colour change

Some animals are experts at changing colour, either to blend in or to scare off predators or rivals. Chameleons and octopuses change colour as their mood or environment changes.

Made for moving

Most animals move to find food or shelter, escape danger, find a mate and care for young. Their bodies are built for movement, whether they run, fly or swim.

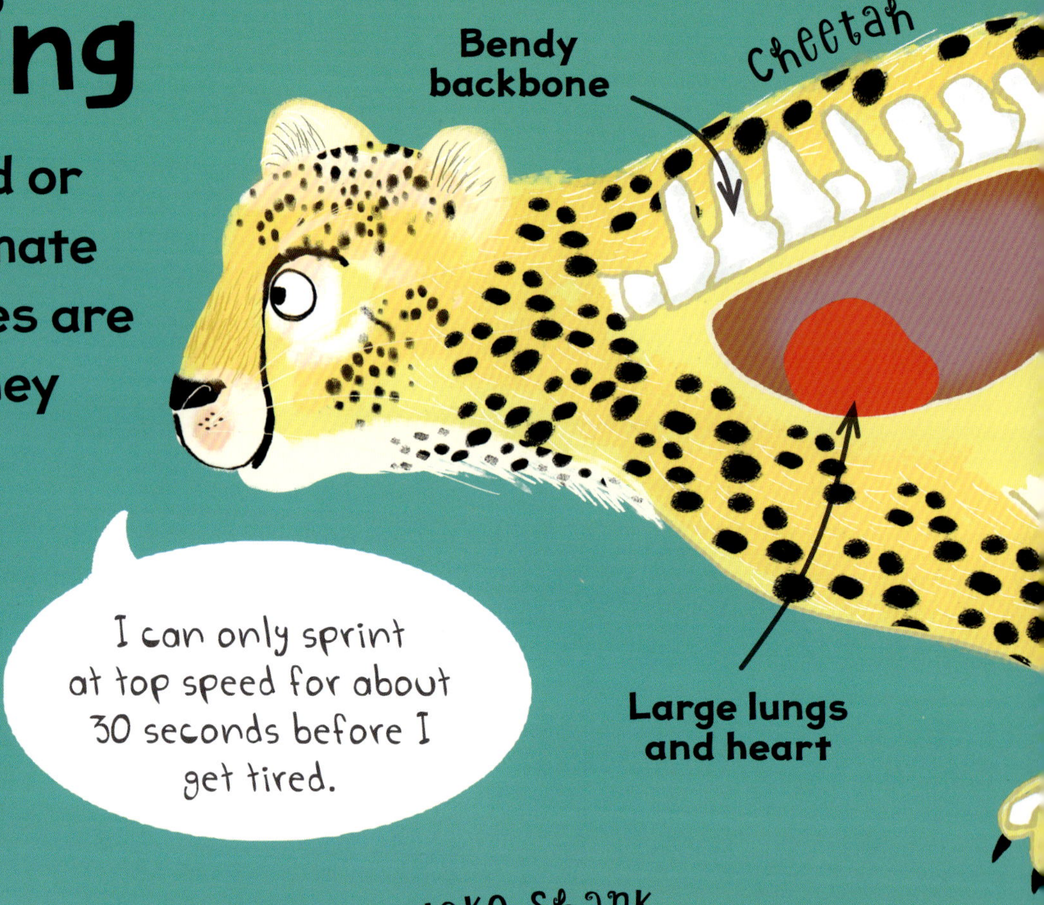

Speed champion

Many predators chase their prey. The cheetah is the fastest land animal over short distances, sprinting at up to 100 kilometres an hour.

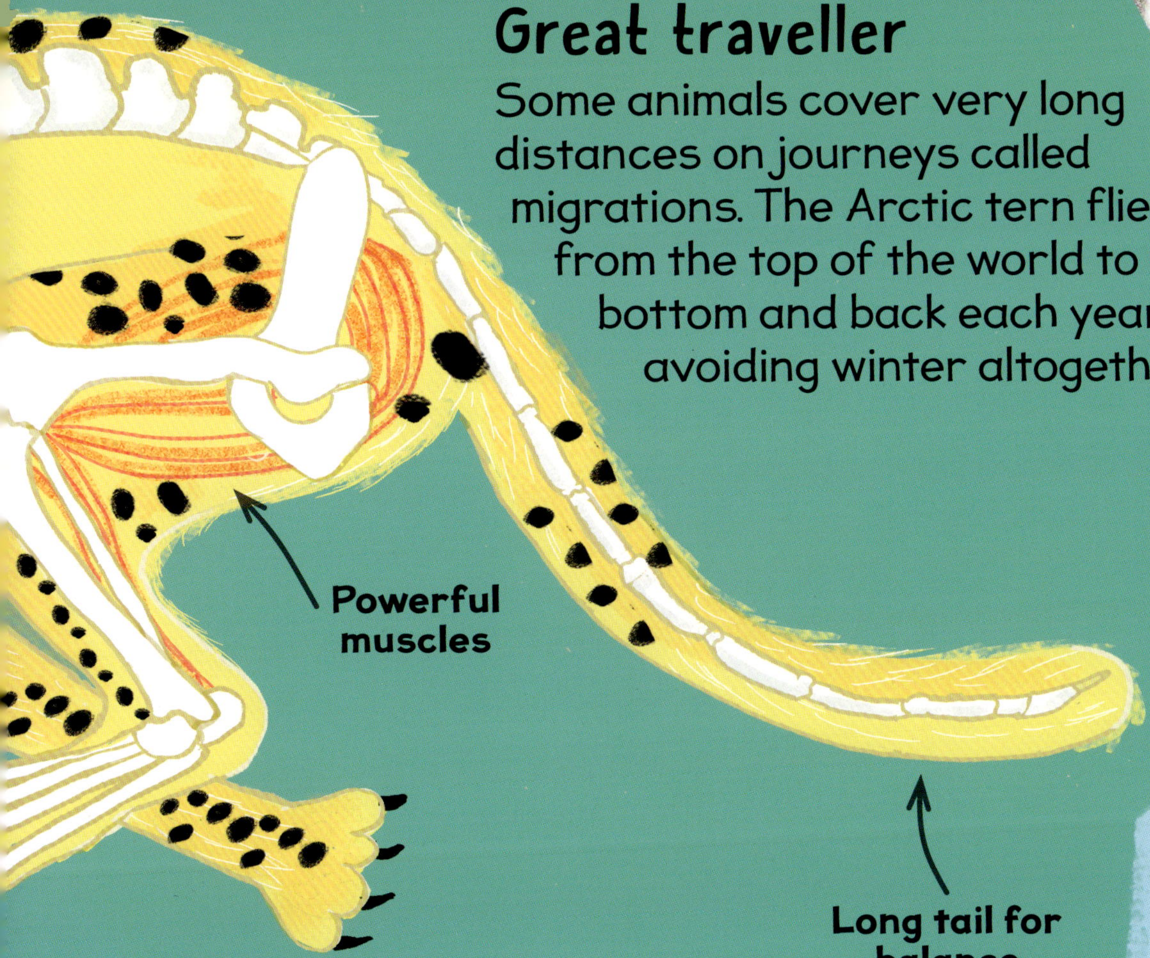

Great traveller

Some animals cover very long distances on journeys called migrations. The Arctic tern flies from the top of the world to the bottom and back each year, avoiding winter altogether.

I CAN... MOVE LIKE AN ANIMAL

See if you and your friends can move like these animals: a sprinting cheetah, a slithering snake, a stalking tiger, a hopping frog, a bounding kangaroo, a crab scuttling sideways.

Many millipedes have 300 legs, or more!

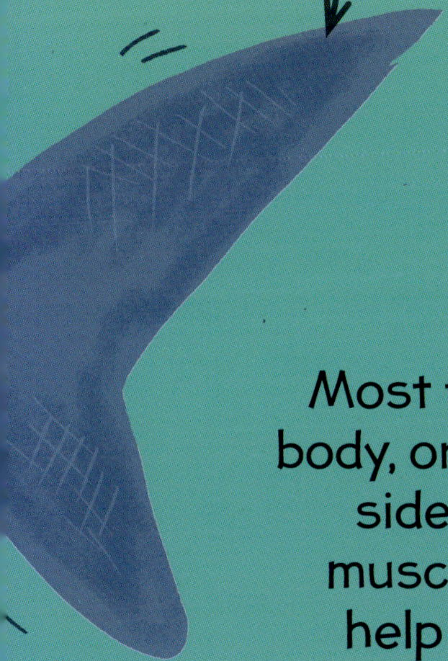

Fishy tales

Most fish swim by bending their body, or just their tail, from side to side. Fast fish have powerful muscles and a smooth shape to help them glide through water.

An eagle tears up meat with its hooked bill

Hungry animals

All animals need to eat to live. Omnivores, such as foxes, eat almost anything. Herbivores, such as hares, eat only plants. Carnivores like eagles just eat meat. Food chains show how animals are linked by what they eat.

Hares have teeth that never stop growing. Gnawing on tough plants wears them down.

Plants are always at the bottom of the food chain, as they use sunlight to make their own food

Animal cutlery

To break up solid food, some animals use their teeth or jaws and some birds use their bills. Many insects suck up liquid food with special mouthparts.

Giant anteaters flick out their long **tongues** at up to 160 times per minute as they feed.

I CAN... DRAW FOOD CHAINS

Try putting these things in the right order to create a food chain. Think about what eats what. The answer is on page 48.

grasshopper • grass snake
frog • grass

Packing a punch

Some types of mantis shrimp have club-like claws that can unfold and strike prey at lightning speed.

Predators and prey

Predators hunt, catch and eat other animals, which are called their prey. They use weapons such as big teeth, powerful jaws, sharp claws, sticky tongues and poison.

A mantis shrimp's punch is so powerful it can smash glass!

Hidden danger

Cunning predators may set traps. Some trapdoor spiders grab their prey from behind a kind of door at their burrow entrance.

I CAN... GO FISHING

Draw lots of fish onto card and colour them in. Cut them out and fix a metal paper clip to each one. Put the fish into a bowl. Tie magnets to chopsticks or lolly sticks and use them as fishing rods. How many fish can you catch?

Fighting back

Prey animals defend themselves with teeth, claws or spines. They may also use tricks. The frilled lizard opens its neck frill to look big and scary to predators.

Fantastic features

Some animals have amazing body features such as horns, curly tails or long feathers. These can help them to move, escape danger or win a mate.

Impressive antlers

Male animals use their antlers, tusks or horns to fight for females. Male deer start to grow a new set of antlers every spring. They are fully grown by the autumn mating season.

Weird and wonderful

Most lizards can break off their tails to escape predators. The tail slowly grows back.

The healthiest deer have the biggest antlers.

Ribbon-tailed astrapia

I CAN… MAKE ANTLERS

For each antler, take a pipe cleaner and twist three more around it, pointing upwards. Wrap strips of newspaper around the antlers and cover with masking tape. Twist the bottom ends around a headband – now they're ready to wear!

The hooded seal blows up a red 'balloon' from its nostril to help attract a mate and warn rivals.

Sugar gliders can glide through the air using 'wings' of thin skin.

Hold on tight

The special gripping tails of spider monkeys, seahorses and tree snakes curl tightly around a support to hold it in place.

Super senses

Animals usually collect information about their surroundings using their senses of sight, hearing, smell, taste and touch. Keen senses help animals to survive.

Lots of lenses

A dragonfly has enormous eyes. Each eye is made up of about 30,000 tiny lenses joined together.

Fantastic feelers

Some animals sense the world in a different way from us. Butterflies and moths smell with their feelers, called antennae. They also taste with their feet.

Invisible ears

Mammals have ear flaps outside their head. Other animals just have inside ears. The dish-like shape of a barn owl's face helps to direct sounds to its inside ears.

I CAN... COLLECT SOUNDS

Ask an adult to find a safe place for you to sit outside and then tie a blindfold around your eyes. Sit still and listen to all the sounds around you for about five minutes. Your hearing will be more sensitive with your eyes covered. How many different sounds can you hear?

I have an extra sense! Sharks like me have tiny holes full of jelly on our heads and snouts. These sense electricity given off by other animals.

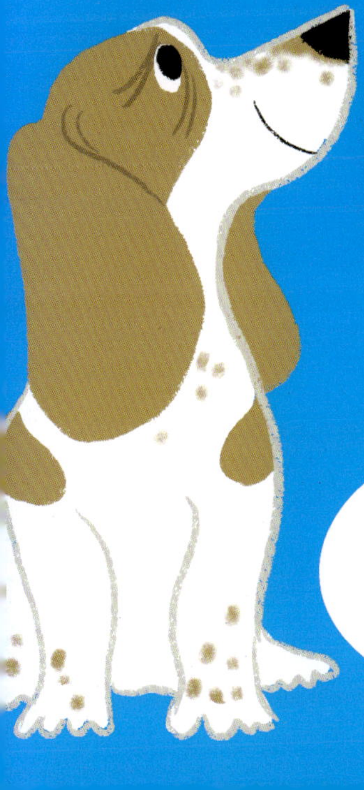

Chameleons can move each eye in a different direction at the same time to see all around.

A dog's sense of smell is about 100,000 times better than yours!

Night life

If you sleep during the day and are active at night, you're nocturnal. Animals that are nocturnal can avoid daytime heat and predators. There is also less competition for food, as there are fewer nocturnal animals than daytime ones.

Each spotted hyena has its own unique whooping call. It can use it to find other members of its clan in the dark.

Bouncing back

Bats make high-pitched sounds and listen for the echoes that bounce back from objects. This is called echolocation. It helps the bat to hunt and find its way.

I CAN... WATCH MOTHS AT NIGHT

When it gets dark, ask an adult to help you hang an old white sheet on a washing line, or over a branch. Turn off any lights and shine a torch or bright lamp onto the sheet. Wait for the moths to be attracted to the light!

Sounds and signals

There are many different sounds and signals that animals use to pass on messages. This is called communication. Animals usually communicate with each other to show where food is, attract a mate or give a warning.

Sounds are very important for animals that live in forests, where it's difficult to see each other.

The cries of howler monkeys can be heard up to 5 kilometres away.

Horrible howls

Howler monkeys are one of the noisiest land animals. Their booming howls warn other howler monkey groups to keep out of their area. This helps to avoid fights.

Wiggle waggle

Honey bees perform a 'waggle dance' to show others in the hive where a good patch of flowers is.

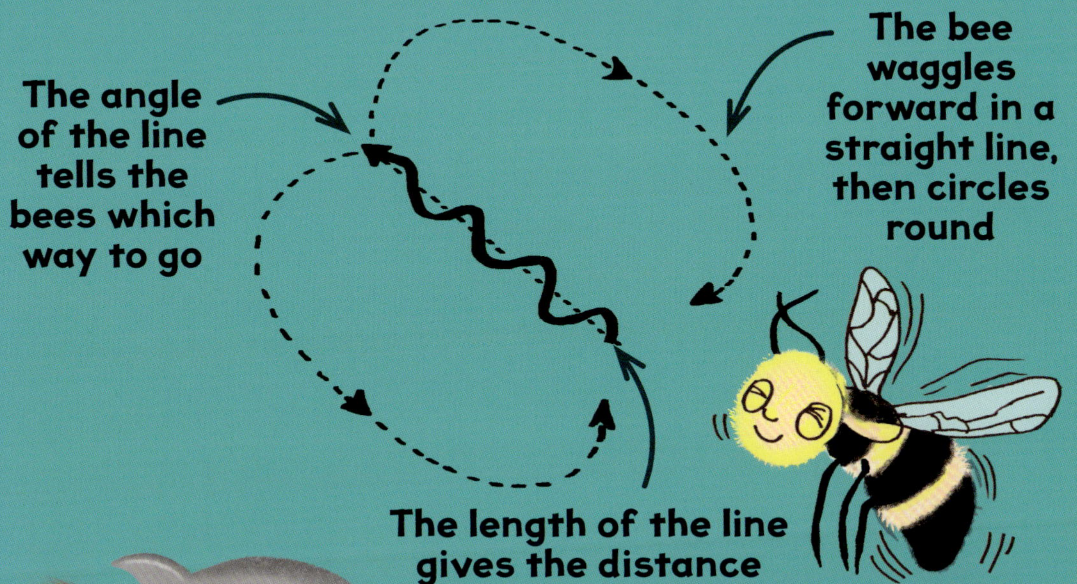

Wolf talk

Wolves are very intelligent, and can 'talk' using growls, whimpers, whines and barks. They also use scent and body language to communicate.

I CAN... MATCH ANIMAL SOUNDS

dolphin

scorpion

See if you can match each animal with a sound that it makes to communicate. The answers are on page 48.

llama

horse

Hisssss

Hummm

Click click

Neiiiiigh

Living in groups

Animals that live in groups help each other to find food, watch out for danger and bring up the young. Group living also helps animals to cope with changes.

Elephant seal pups

Our parents leave us safely together in 'nurseries' when they go off to find food.

Safety in numbers

Some animals, such as penguins and seals, live in groups only for the breeding season. Many adults can keep a sharper look out for predators.

Termites attack the twig inside the mound, then we pull it out to eat them.

Watch and learn

Young animals in a group learn by copying the adults. Chimps learn how to get termites out of a mound by watching an adult 'fish' with a stem or twig.

Up to five million termites live inside one termite mound.

I CAN... NAME ANIMAL GROUPS

Groups of certain animals are given names. Here are some particularly strange ones:

A caravan of camels
A cauldron of bats
A crash of rhinos
A creep of tortoises
A fever of stingrays
A gaggle of geese
A leap of leopards
A murder of crows
A parliament of owls
A shiver of sharks

Newborn babies

Baby animals either hatch out of eggs or are born from their mother's body. Mothers that give birth to babies protect and feed them inside their bodies until they are ready to be born.

When the babies are ready to hatch, they make a chirping noise. The mother opens the nest

Nile crocodiles dig their nests in sand, close to water

The mother lays 40–60 eggs, then covers the nest

Whether a crocodile becomes a male or a female depends on the temperature of the nest.

Cosy nests

Animals that lay eggs often build nests to keep them safe. The warmth of a nest also helps the eggs to develop more quickly.

The female star-fingered toad carries her eggs under the skin of her back until they hatch.

I CAN... MIX AND MATCH

See if you can match these mixed-up babies and parents. The answers are on page 48.

bobcat • cub
deer • cygnet
echidna • pup
emu • kitten
goose • calf
hippo • gosling
lion • chick
shark • puggle
swan • fawn

Magic purse

Most fish lay eggs. Shark eggs are protected by special cases, often called mermaid's purses. Some sharks give birth to babies, called pups.

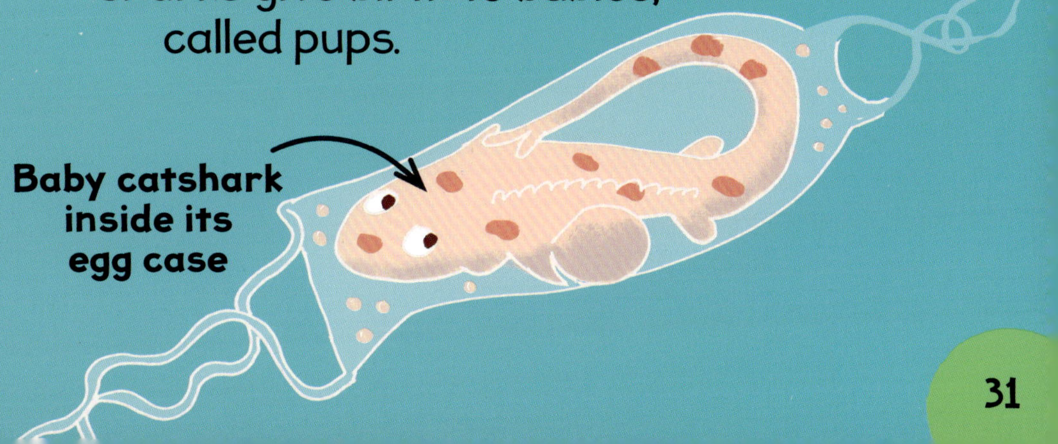

Growing up

Some young animals, such as snakes or orangutans, look like their parents. Others, such as frogs, look very different at first. They change as they grow up.

1 Female frogs lay jelly-covered eggs underwater

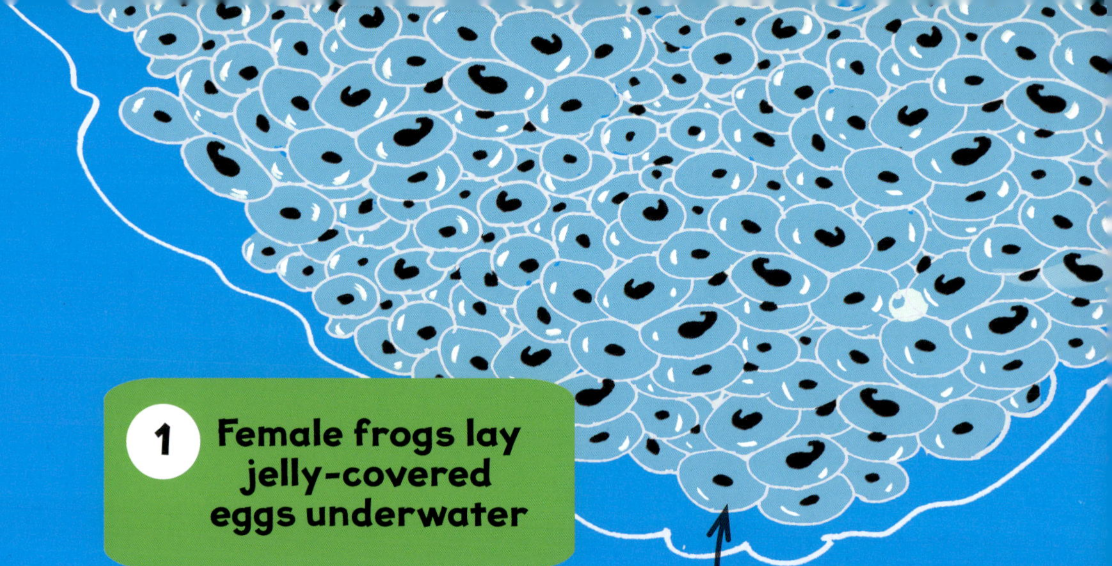

Frog eggs are called frogspawn. The frog lays them in large clumps

2 A tiny tadpole hatches from each egg. It can breathe underwater through flaps called gills

3 The tadpole gets bigger. Its back legs start to grow

4 The front legs grow. Over time, the tail gets shorter

Pocket baby

Animals with pouches, such as kangaroos and wombats, are called marsupials. Their babies are tiny when they are born and grow slowly inside their mother's pouch.

Inside the pouch, I feed on my mum's milk.

A baby kangaroo is small enough to fit onto a teaspoon when it is born!

I CAN... RECORD MY HEIGHT

Stick a long, thin piece of paper on a wall or door (ask an adult first). Mark your height on it with your age as you grow up. You can even decorate your height chart!

On land, I breathe air through lungs. My gills have disappeared.

5 **The tadpole has become a froglet, and has left the water**

6 **The froglet grows into an adult frog**

Safe homes

A home can give animals shelter, protection from predators and a place to store food and have a family. Many animals build their homes.

Weaving wonder

Male weaverbirds make a nest by weaving together grass, stems and leaves. The nests have narrow entrances that face down, so predators can't get in.

A **hummingbird's** cup-shaped nest is only about the size of a table tennis ball.

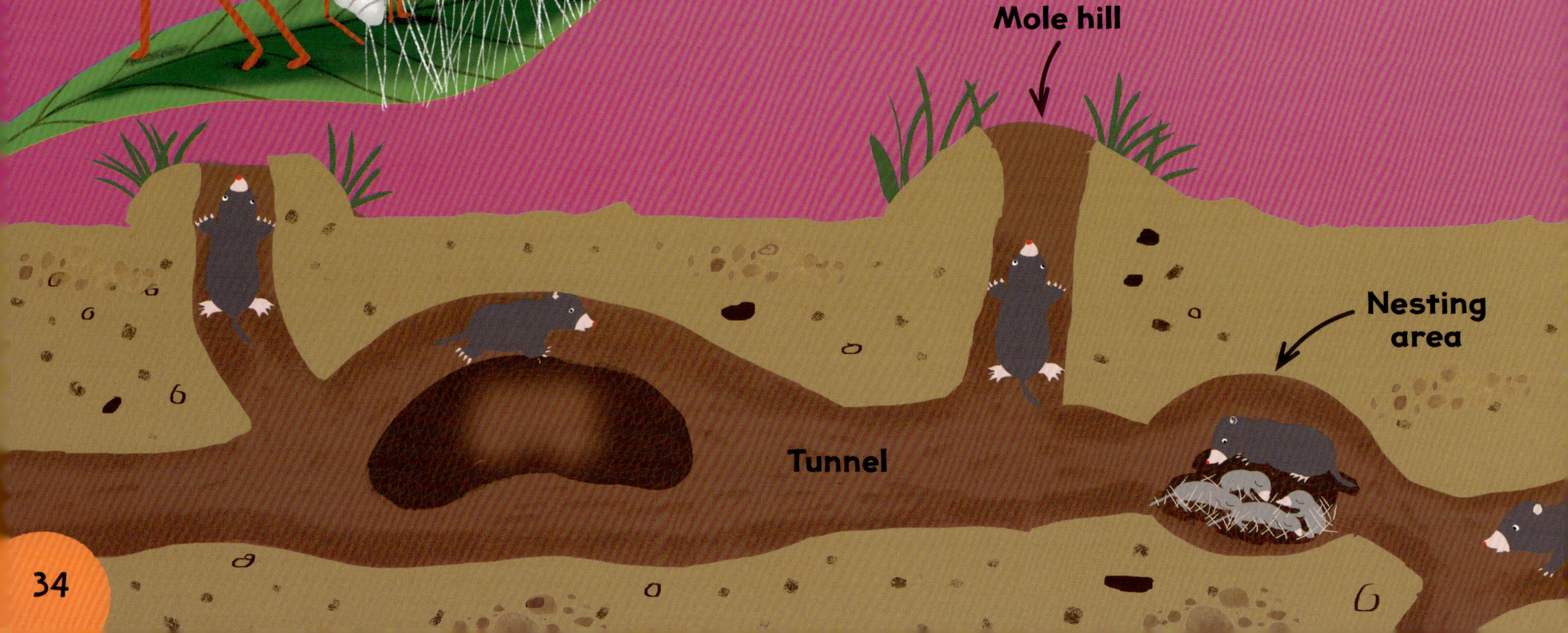

Treetop tower

Some animals build a new home each year. Others keep the same home but make improvements. Bald eagles add more sticks to their huge treetop nest every year.

The biggest bald eagle nest weighed more than a rhino!

Champion digger

Animals that build underground homes are very good diggers. Moles dig tunnels with their long nails and spade-like hands, which are linked to strong chest muscles.

I CAN... MAKE A GIANT NEST

Collect some soft and warm objects, such as cushions, pillows, rugs and duvets, from around your home. Find a big space and arrange them to make a giant nest.

Out in the cold

In Earth's coldest places, animals have thick fur or feathers and fatty blubber to keep them warm. Small, round ears also help to stop an animal's body heat escaping.

During the harsh Antarctic winter, emperor penguins form giant huddles for warmth. They take turns to be on the outside!

Ice fish have a chemical 'anti-freeze' in their blood. This keeps them from freezing solid in Antarctic waters.

I CAN... DRESS FOR SNOW

Dress up as if you are going out to play in the snow. Lots of thin layers are warmer than just one thick one, because each layer traps some warm air from your body, just like a penguin's feathers.

Snow paws

A polar bear's huge paws work like snowshoes to stop it sinking. The undersides of the paws are rough to stop the bear slipping. Its sharp claws provide extra grip.

Too hot to handle

In hot, dry deserts, many animals hide from the daytime heat and get most of their water from their food. Reptiles can thrive in deserts because they have watertight bodies and can go without food for a long time.

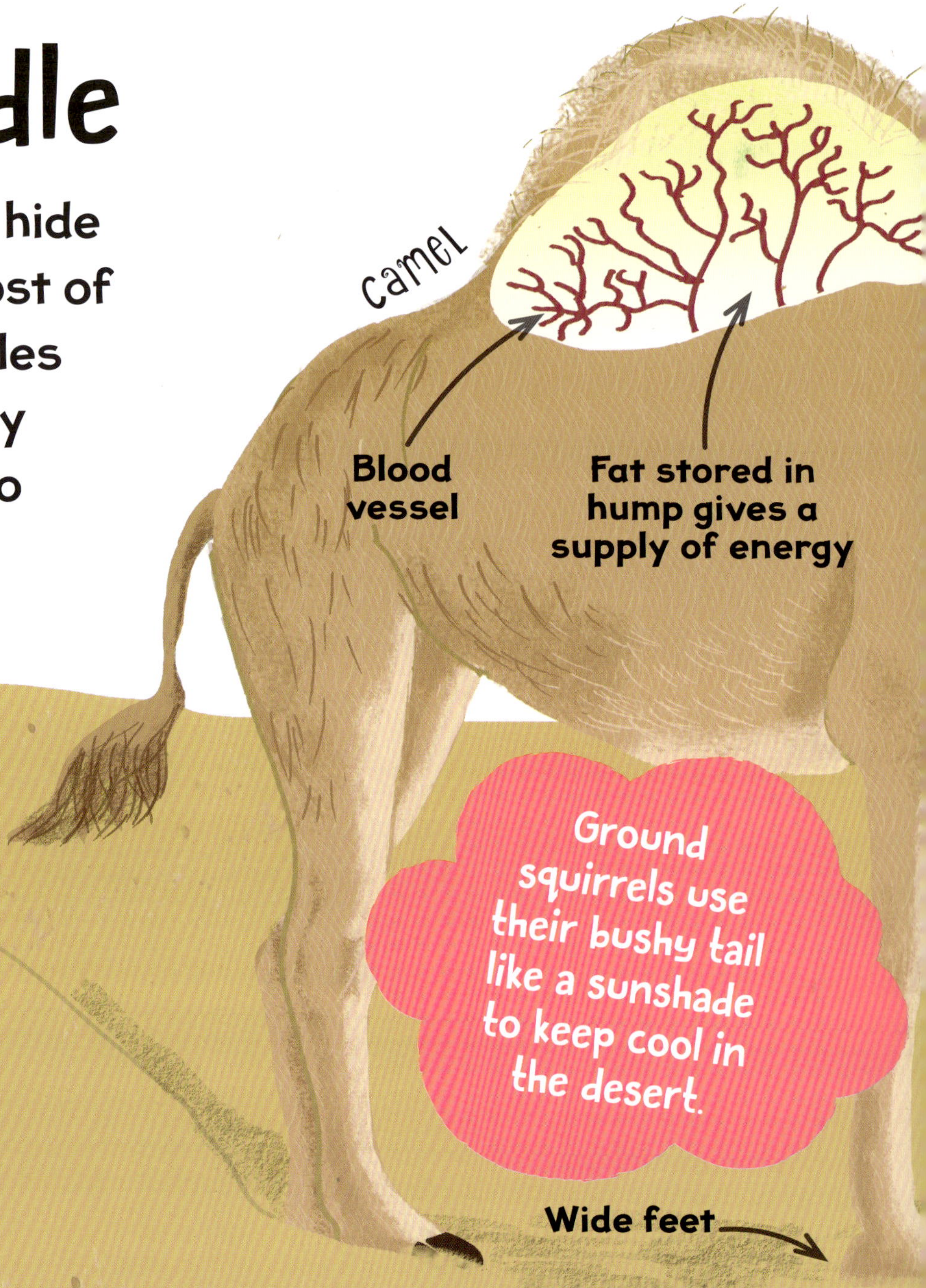

Scorpions can survive without water for several months.

Ground squirrels use their bushy tail like a sunshade to keep cool in the desert.

Sand swimmer

It's hard to move across very hot, soft sand, so the sandfish (a type of lizard) burrows underneath. It swims through the sand like a fish swimming through water.

Desert expert

Larger animals, such as camels, have to travel far to find food and water. Long legs help them to cover the ground and wide feet stop them sinking into the sand.

I CAN... WALK LIKE A CAMEL

Ask an adult for help. Cut out some big circles of plastic (from the recycling). Make holes in the bottoms and tie them on your feet with string. If you walk on soft sand or soil, your big feet will stop you sinking.

Slimy parcel

To avoid drying out, the water-holding frog burrows underground and forms a slimy cocoon around itself, which holds water. When the rains arrive, the frog emerges and tears open the cocoon.

Life in the trees

Forest habitats provide animals with plenty of shelter and food. But in cooler forests, the long cold winters provide many challenges. Some animals sleep through the winter or travel to warmer places.

Agile acrobats

Many forest animals are strong climbers. Squirrels have powerful legs and sharp claws to cling to trees. They use their bushy tail to steer and balance as they leap.

I CAN... MAKE WILD ART

Hundreds of animals depend on one tree for food and shelter. Collect sticks, leaves and flowers and create a wild art picture of a tree on the ground. Place toy animals in the tree or make your own animals to complete your picture.

Sleepyhead

Dormice sleep through the cold winter months in a warm nest. They eat a lot during the autumn and build up stores of body fat to help them survive the long winter.

Amazing oceans

Our planet has much more water than dry land. Animals live in the salty oceans and the freshwater of rivers and lakes. The oceans are full of life, from the sunny surface waters to the inky black depths.

Tube worms up to 2.4 metres long live around very hot cracks in the deep ocean floor.

Stay in school

In the ocean, there are few places to hide. Many fish swim in large groups, called shoals or schools. This helps the fish to protect themselves from predators and swim more easily.

Coral reefs are home to an incredible variety of sea creatures. There are plenty of food and hiding places on a reef.

I CAN... THINK ABOUT STAYING SAFE

There is safety in numbers for schools of fish. Which activities do you prefer to do in a group with friends or family? In a scary situation, would you rather be in a group or on your own?

Breathing underwater

Fish take in oxygen from the water through thin flaps called gills. A fish's gills have blood passing through them. The blood picks up the oxygen and carries it around the fish's body.

Water worlds

Animals thrive in freshwater habitats. There is plenty of food in rivers and lakes and lots of places for birds and mammals to nest and raise their young.

Tiny insects called Pond skaters can walk on water without sinking.

I CAN... DISCOVER WATER ANIMALS

Ask an adult to take you on a pond dipping trip or to explore rock pools at the seaside. Remember to put any animals you find back where they came from.

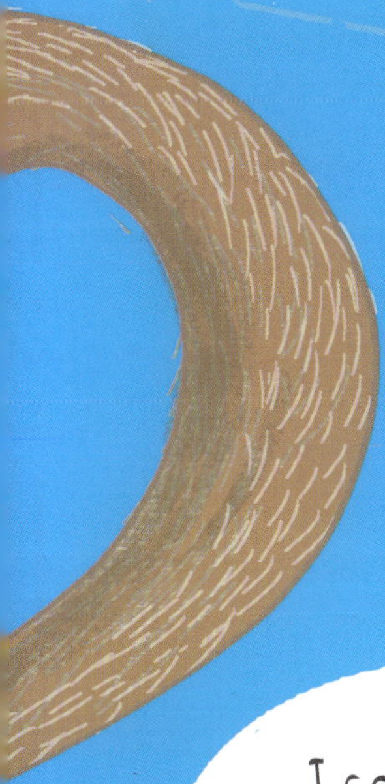

Flipper feet

Some water animals, such as otters, have skin between their toes. They use their webbed feet to push against the water and swim faster, rather like a person wearing flippers.

Save our rivers!

People pollute rivers, take too many fish and build dams, which block the flow of water. This threatens the survival of many freshwater animals, such as the rare Mekong giant catfish.

Animals at risk

Many animals are in danger of dying out because of things people do. The biggest threats are habitats being destroyed, pollution, hunting, wars and animals being illegally sold. But many people are working hard to save at risk animals.

Protecting chimps

The Jane Goodall Institute works to protect chimpanzees in Tanzania, East Africa.

They work with chimps in their forest homes.

Plastic peril

Some sea turtles eat plastic bags, as they think they are jellyfish.

It's up to all of us to create less waste, so less ends up in the ocean.

Rhino recovery

Huge numbers of black rhinos were hunted for their horns. They are now protected and their numbers have doubled since 1995.

Good news for pandas

Larger, protected nature reserves have been created for wild giant pandas to live in.

Pandas born in captivity are now being released into the wild.

Super science

The more scientists understand about animals, the more they are able to protect them. This whale shark is being tagged so scientists can track its movements.

I CAN... HELP RARE ANIMALS

Join or follow the WWF (World Wide Fund for Nature) to find out more about rare animals and how to save them. You could also adopt or sponsor a rare animal at your local zoo or wildlife park.

Test your memory

Now it's time to find out what you've learnt. The information to answer these questions can all be found on the main pages.

1. What is the name for an animal without a backbone?
2. Which animal is the biggest ever to have lived on our planet?
3. What is the word for colours and patterns that help animals to hide?
4. Which is the fastest land animal?
5. Which tiny animals do giant anteaters eat?
6. What are the feelers on an insect's head called?
7. What is the name for animals that are active at night?
8. Which newborn animal is small enough to fit onto a teaspoon?
9. What is the name for the fat under a penguin's skin?
10. How do sandgrouse collect water?

I CAN... ANSWERS

Page 17
grass → grasshopper → frog → grass snake

Page 27
dolphin Click click
llama Hummm
scorpion Hisssss
horse Neiiiiigh

Page 31
bobcat • kitten
deer • fawn
echidna • puggle
emu • chick
goose • gosling
hippo • calf
lion • cub
shark • pup
swan • cygnet

ANSWERS

1. Invertebrate
2. Blue whale
3. Camouflage
4. Cheetah
5. Ants and termites
6. Antennae
7. Nocturnal
8. Kangaroo
9. Blubber
10. By using their feathers to soak it up